Laura Ingalls Wilder's
Fairy Poems

Laura Ingalls Wilder's

Fairy Poems

Introduced and compiled by
STEPHEN W. HINES

Illustrated by
RICHARD HULL

Doubleday

For Merry
S.W.H.

For my daughter, Carrie
R.H.

CONTENTS

LAURA INGALLS WILDER
Her Story

BY STEPHEN W. HINES

THE YEAR 1915 WAS PIVOTAL FOR MRS. Almanzo James Wilder, the woman who was to become better known as Laura Ingalls Wilder, the beloved children's author. Wilder's husband agreed to stay and run their farm in the Missouri Ozarks as she headed west for a long trip to California. Such a journey was unusual for a wife of that time, but Wilder wanted to visit her married daughter, Rose Wilder Lane, who had settled and was working in San Francisco.

Wilder also wanted to pursue her lifelong dream of becoming a writer of fiction.

Rose Wilder Lane was already a successful newspaper writer, doing articles for the *San Francisco Bulletin* about the opportunities opening up for women in the modern era. Laura Ingalls Wilder wanted to learn from Rose so that she could write about her own experiences growing up on the prairie in Kansas, Minnesota, and South Dakota.

At that time, Wilder had yet to create her now classic *Little*

1

House on the Prairie characters Ma and Pa Ingalls, Carrie and Grace and Mary, and Jack the bulldog. If Wilder had not traveled west, we probably would not have spent countless hours reading about their adventures or watching the long-running television program of the same name.

Wilder wasn't a total novice as a writer. She had already been writing for a farm paper that was eager to run her how-to articles on housekeeping and chicken farming, but she aspired to greater things.

Rose broadened her mother's education. She escorted Wilder around bustling San Francisco, introduced her to a wide variety of writers and artists, and showed her the workings of a great city newspaper. Wilder drank it all in.

During a two-month period, mother and daughter were inseparable, and it seems certain that seeds were planted that later blossomed into Wilder's stories for children. We know that Rose continued to offer writing advice and help throughout her mother's career.

The collection of fairy poems in this book came about from the happy collaboration that had begun to develop between mother and daughter. Rose was writing occasional poetry for a *San Francisco Bulletin* feature called the "Tuck 'em In Corner," but she was too busy with other projects to spend much time on it. Wilder, who loved to write poetry, seized the opportunity for herself.

Choosing fairies as her subject, Wilder found a delightful diversion from the pieces on poultry she was beginning to write for the *St. Louis Post-Dispatch* and other papers. Her Ozark woods were full of quail and deer, shady bowers, and babbling streams. The wild forest flowers provided just the right inspiration for her to find the invisible fairy folk who made the flowers and woods their home.

The editors of the *San Francisco Bulletin* readily published Wilder's fairy poems, little realizing they were giving a start to the woman who would become the most popular American children's author of all time.

Fairies Still Appear to Those with Seeing Eyes

by Laura Ingalls Wilder

Adapted from an essay written in 1916

HAVE YOU SEEN ANY FAIRIES lately? I asked the question of a little girl not long ago. "Huh! There's no such thing as fairies," she replied. In some way the answer hurt me, and I have been vaguely disquieted when I have thought of it ever since.

In the long, long ago days, when the farmers gathered their crops, they always used to leave a part of whatever crop they were harvesting in or on the ground for the use of the "Little People."

This was fair, for the "Little People" worked hard in the ground to help the farmer grow his crops, and if a share were not left for them, they became angry and the crops would not be good the next year. You may laugh at this old superstition, but I leave it to you if it has not been proven true that where the "Little People" of the soil are not fed the crops are poor.

Dryads used to live in the trees, you know—beautiful, fairy creatures who now and then were glimpsed beside the tree in which they vanished. There have been long years during which we have heard nothing of them, but now scientists have discovered that the leaves of trees have eyes, actual eyes that mirror surrounding objects.

Of what use are eyes to a tree, I wonder? Would it not be fine if scientists gave us back all our fairies under different names?

I have a feeling that childhood has been robbed of a great deal of its joys by taking away its belief in wonderful, mystic things, in fairies and all their kin. It is not surprising that when children are grown, they have so little idealism or imagination, nor that so many of them are like the infidel who asserted that he would not believe anything that he could not see.

The Quaker made a good retort, "Friend! Does thee believe thee has any brains?"

By the way, have *you* seen any fairies lately? Please do not answer as the little girl did, for I'm sure there are fairies and that you at least have seen their work.

Laura Ingalls Wilder's

Fairy Poems

The Fairy Dew Drop

Down by the spring one morning
Where the shadows still lay deep,
I found in the heart of a flower
A tiny fairy asleep.

Her flower couch was perfumed,
Leaf curtains drawn with care,
And there she sweetly slumbered,
With a jewel in her hair.

But a sunbeam entered softly
And touched her, as she lay,
Whispering that 'twas morning
And fairies must away.

All colors of the rainbow
Were in her robe so bright
As she danced away with the sunbeam
And vanished from my sight.

'Twas while I watched them dancing,
The sunshine told me true
That my sparkling little fairy
Was lovely Drop O' Dew.*

FEBRUARY 1915

* Drop O' Dew is the Fairy who helps take care of the flowers. All night she carries drink to the thirsty blossoms, bathes the heads of those who have the headache from the heat of the day before, straightens them up on their stems, and makes their colors bright for the morning.

The Fairies in the Sunshine

The little sunshine fairies
Are out on sunny days.
They gaily go a-dancing
Along the country ways.

They paint the flower faces,
The leaves of forest trees,
And tint the little grasses
All waving in the breeze.

(One painting tiger lilies,
Who runs away and goes
To play awhile with baby,
Puts speckles on his nose!!)

They color all the apples
And work for days and weeks
To make the grapes bloom purple
And paint the peaches' cheeks.

Ah! There's a tiny fairy!
She's in the garden bed!
It's little Ray O' Sunshine
Who makes the roses red.

MARCH 1915

Naughty Four O'Clocks

There were some naughty flowers once,
Who were careless in their play;
They got their petals torn and soiled
As they swung in the dust all day.

Then went to bed at four o'clock,
With faces covered tight,
To keep the fairy Drop O' Dew
From washing them at night.

Poor Drop O' Dew! What could she do?
She said to the Fairy Queen,
"I cannot get those Four O'Clocks
To keep their faces clean."

The mighty Storm King heard the tale;
"My winds and rain," roared he,
"Shall wash those naughty flowers well,
As flowers all should be."

So raindrops came and caught them all
Before they went to bed,
And washed those little Four O'Clocks
At three o'clock instead.

APRIL 1915

When Sunshine Fairies Rest

The fairies in the sunshine
Have many things to do.
They are busy night and day,
But have their rest time, too.

For always in the sunlight
They do their very best,
But when the day is cloudy
The sunshine fairies rest.

They go to sleep on soft clouds
A-float around the sun
And tuck their toes in cloudlets,
Until their nap is done.

So when the day is rainy
The dull sky overhead
Is just the soft gray curtain,
Around their downy bed.

Then when their rest is over,
Just as the clouds go by,
They all come out together—
The rainbow in the sky!

MARCH 1915

Where Sunshine Fairies Go

The sunshine fairies cannot rest,
When evening bells are rung;
Nor can they sleep in flowers
When bedtime songs are sung.

They are such busy fairies,
Their work is never done,
For all around and round the world
They travel with the sun.

And while you're soundly sleeping,
They do the best they can
A-painting cherry blossoms
In far away Japan.

The poppy fields of China,
With blossoms bright and gay,
They color on their journey—
And then pass on their way.

And all the happy children,
In islands of the sea,
Know little Ray O' Sunshine,
Who plays with you and me.

MARCH 1915

39

A Doubleday Book
BANTAM DOUBLEDAY DELL PUBLISHING GROUP, INC.
1540 Broadway, New York, New York 10036

Doubleday and the portrayal of an anchor with a dolphin are trademarks of
Bantam Doubleday Dell Publishing Group, Inc.
Introduction and compilation copyright © 1998 by Stephen W. Hines
Illustrations copyright © 1998 by Richard Hull

Library of Congress Cataloging-in-Publication Data

Wilder, Laura Ingalls, 1867–1957.
Laura Ingalls Wilder's fairy poems / compiled by Stephen W. Hines ;
illustrated by Richard Hull.
p.   cm.
"A Doubleday book for young readers"
Contents: Fairy dew drop—Fairies in the sunshine—Naughty four o'clocks—
When sunshine fairies rest—Where sunshine fairies go.
ISBN 0-385-32533-9
1. Fairy poetry, American.   2. Children's poetry, American.
[1. Fairies—poetry.   2. American poetry.]   I. Hines, Stephen W.   II. Hull, Richard, ill.
III. Title.   IV. Title: Fairy poems
PS3545.I342A6   1998a   .   97-27878
811' .52—dc21   CIP
                                               AC

The text of this book is set in Centaur MT and Pabst L.   Book design by Semadar Megged
Manufactured in the United States of America   November 1998
10 9 8 7 6 5 4 3 2 1
BVG